BOOK NEWS

Sign up for exclusive updates and offers at
news.jljarvis.com

CHRISTMAS BY
LAMPLIGHT

CHRISTMAS BY LAMPLIGHT

A HOLIDAY NOVELETTE

J.L. JARVIS

Christmas by Lamplight

ISBN (ebook) 978-1-942767-89-3
ISBN (paperback) 978-1-942767-90-9

Published by Bookbinder Press
bookbinderpress.com

CHAPTER ONE

CARRIE WATSON WAS in love with a voice.

Not in love, she corrected herself, steadying the stepladder against the memoir shelf. That would be pathetic. She was . . . objectively appreciative of rich vocal resonance, evocative delivery, and impeccable pacing.

The earbuds delivered another line of honey-dark baritone directly to her limbic system, and she forgot what she was supposed to be shelving. Always chapter twenty-nine, when he confesses, "I loved Estella with the love of a man, I loved her simply because I found her irresistible," and that velvet-dark voice made the word "irresistible" sound like a sin and a promise all at once. "I loved her against reason," the voice said, "against promise, against peace, against hope, against happiness, against all discouragement that could be."

Carrie's eyes fluttered shut, one hand pressed against her sternum, where her heart was performing acrobatics that would raise a cardiologist's eyebrows.

The bell over the door tried to ring, got stuck, then surrendered with a grunt.

"Oh, no. Let me guess. Chapter twenty-nine?" Shannon Wade walked in, wielding two coffee cups like weapons against the December cold. "It really should come with a black box warning: Do not operate heavy machinery or climb ladders with Tanner Blake narrating *Great Expectations* in your ears."

Carrie yanked out an earbud so fast she nearly toppled off the ladder. "It's inventory assessment."

"Mm-hm." Shannon set the coffees on the counter and assumed her classic position of elbows down, chin in hands, and maximum mischief in her eyes. "The part of the inventory where the hero says he loved her 'with the love of a man'? Brr! I don't know about your assessment, but mine is—"

"Romantic!"

"Oh, yeah! And hazardous. That voice could read a grocery list and cause a soccer mom carpool collision." Shannon slid a cup over. "Speaking of hazards, did you see the email from the landlord?"

Carrie's stomach performed an unpleasant flip. "I saw it."

"Lease renewal: five thousand by December 27, or . . ." Shannon winced.

"I know what 'or' means, Shannon."

"Do you? Because I think 'or' means Ahab Coffee moves in and turns your charming, independent bookshop into franchise number thirteen twenty-seven. And that's just on this block."

Carrie climbed down from the ladder and wrapped her hands around the coffee cup. The shop stretched around them—exposed brick she'd scrubbed herself, mismatched vintage fixtures she'd found at estate sales, and the beautiful old shelving that had come with the space when she'd bought it from the previous owner's bankruptcy sale. Everything had a history. She'd turned someone else's failure into a warm and inviting space, proving she could see potential where others saw loss.

She just hadn't proven she could make it profitable.

Shannon's voice softened. "How bad is it?"

"Bad," Carrie admitted. "I've got a shop full of inventory and no advertising budget. No one knows we exist."

"Well, no, but you've been building your dream."

"I've been proving a point." The words came out sharper than intended. "And now Dennis gets to be right about his predictions."

Shannon's expression darkened at the mention of Carrie's ex. "Dennis is an insufferable ass who told you you'd fail because he needed you to fail. Don't give him that satisfaction."

"Then I need a miracle by December 27."

"We'll make it work. We always do."

They stood in silence, surveying the shop. Carrie had poured everything into these walls—her savings, her pride, her desperate need to prove she was more than Dennis had told her she was for five soul-crushing years. *You're not practical enough. Not business-minded. Too emotional for entrepreneurship.*

She'd left him, found this space, and built something beautiful on her own. But three years in, she was struggling on Hollydale's quiet Main Street.

She just needed people to find it.

The morning routine steadied her—flip the lamps on, start the cocoa station, and arrange the new releases to catch the light. Shannon put on the vintage Christmas playlist with Bing Crosby, Ella Fitzgerald, and Mel Tormé.

Carrie had just climbed back on the ladder to fix the perpetually crooked "Local Authors" shelf when the ancient bookcase creaked and groaned like a cellar door in a haunted Victorian house.

The entire Austen section tilted forward in slow motion.

Carrie lunged for it, knowing she was too far away. She could already see the avalanche of books, broken spines, bent pages, and one more thing on a repair list she couldn't afford to address.

A hand caught the shelf.

Not caught, *commanded* it to stop. One hand steady as stone, while the other pressed against the small of her back to keep her from pitching off the ladder.

"Careful," a voice said.

Carrie's entire body went still. *That voice . . . No, it couldn't be.*

She looked down into eyes the color of strong coffee, and under a beanie was a face that belonged on the cover of Woodworking Quarterly if there were such a thing. The man holding her shelf—and technically her—wore flannel draped over a thermal shirt, muscular shoulders, well-worn jeans that rode low on hips that were . . . not the point right now. The point was the shelf. And not falling. Also breathing, which she needed to do.

His expression of mild concern suggested that rescuing women from literary landslides was just another Tuesday.

"I'll brace this," he said, shifting his weight to pin

the shelf with his shoulder while steadying her. "Unless this is some sort of performance art piece. Falling action? I don't judge."

That was the voice. Low. Controlled. The kind of voice that probably never had to repeat itself. The voice that had carried her through inventory at 2 a.m., through the night she'd finally left Dennis, through every moment when the world felt too big and she felt too small.

"I—no. Thank you. I just—" She gestured with the staple gun she'd been using to fix the bookshelf and accidentally fired it, pinning his sleeve to the shelf.

Shannon made a sound like a stepped-on cat toy.

The man looked at his sleeve, then at her, and the corner of his mouth did something that wasn't quite a smile but made her stomach leap to her throat. "I usually let a woman buy me dinner before we do hardware."

"Oh my gosh. I'm so—let me—" She turned to find Shannon, arm outstretched with a staple remover at the ready, which Carrie took and leaned closer than was professionally appropriate. The faint scent of cedar, sawdust, and fresh snow went to her head, and she thought she might faint. Her fingers fumbled with the staple, but she finally freed him.

"Tanner Blake?" The words came out in a breathless fangirl sigh, exactly what she'd promised herself she would never do.

His expression shifted, not quite to panic, but close. His jaw tightened. For a long moment, he just studied her, and she saw exhaustion, the bone-deep weariness of someone who'd been pushed to his limit.

"While I'm here," he said quietly, "I'd really appreciate it if you'd call me Tom."

The vulnerability in those words hit her square in the chest. This wasn't a celebrity asking for privacy—this was someone asking for refuge. His hand was still pressed against her back, steadying her, but his eyes were asking for something else entirely.

Carrie knew that look. *Please. Just let me be invisible.* She'd worn it herself six months ago, walking away from Dennis with nothing but a suitcase, a backpack, and the keys to a failing bookshop. It was the look of someone who'd been broken and just needed somewhere to heal.

She stepped down from the ladder, and he released her, stepping back like he expected her to demand an explanation—or worse—a selfie.

Instead, she stuck out her hand. "Nice to meet you, Tom. I'm Carrie Watson. I run this place."

He stared at her hand for a beat, then took it. His grip was warm, calloused, careful. The relief in his voice was almost painful. "I just moved in upstairs yesterday."

Their hands lingered a second too long. His thumb brushed against her palm, and the touch sent heat straight up her arm.

Shannon made a strangled sound from behind the counter.

Carrie pulled her hand back and cleared her throat. "Thank you. For the shelf. For not letting me fall."

"Anytime." He crouched to examine the baseboards, his shoulders relaxing incrementally, as though he were only now realizing he was safe.

He ran his hand along the wood and then eyed her

staple gun fix with a skeptical look. "This needs to be properly repaired. Soon. You saw what just happened. That shelf's one bump away from coming down on a customer. You don't want a lawsuit on your hands."

Heat crept up her neck. "Yeah, I know. It's on the list. It'll have to wait until I can afford to get a carpenter in here."

"I can fix it." He said it simply, like it wasn't a big deal.

"I can't let you do that. You're—" She stopped herself before she could say *famous* or a *celebrity* or anything else in her mind that would make this more awkward. "I can't just have you fix things for free."

"Why not?"

"Because it's—it's too much to ask."

"You didn't ask. I offered—because I can, and you need it fixed." He looked at her with those expressive eyes, and there was gratitude in his expression, maybe, for not making this harder than it had to be. Or maybe he just needed a normal task to do, useful work that had nothing to do with the world's expectations.

Carrie wanted to argue, if not out of pride, then to maintain some shred of professional distance. But the way he was looking at her, like this mattered to him somehow, made her pride and professionalism dissolve.

"Okay," she said finally. "Tom. Thank you."

His shoulders dropped another fraction. "I'll grab my tools."

"You have tools?" The question came out before she could stop it.

The corner of his mouth twitched. "Yeah. Wood-working's kind of a hobby. It's what I do between jobs to decompress."

"You decompress by building things?"

"It's better than tearing them down." He said it lightly, but there seemed to be meaning behind the words.

He left, footsteps fading up the back stairs to the second-floor apartment. Shannon grabbed Carrie's arm hard enough to leave a handprint.

"That's Tanner Blake," she hissed.

"I know."

"*The* Tanner Blake. In our shop. Offering to fix our shelf."

"I know."

"And you just agreed to call him Tom!"

"He's hiding from something. I'm not going to make it worse." Carrie pulled her arm free and started straightening books. "The last thing he needs is my making a big deal about who he is."

"You basically told him you're in love with his voice."

Carrie's jaw dropped in protest. "I did not!"

"'Nice to meet you?'"

"What's wrong with that? It's what polite people say."

Shannon raised an eyebrow. "It wasn't the words. It was your face."

"My face was being polite."

"Your face was doing things—things that said I love you, and let's name our children. Please don't name them Pip and Estella." Shannon studied her. "Do you even know why he's hiding?"

"Does it matter? He asked for privacy. I'm giving it to him."

Tanner returned with a toolbox that looked like it

had seen actual use—worn handle, scratched metal, and battle scars earned in the field, not just purchased for a manly appearance. He set it down and got to work with focused intensity.

Carrie tried not to watch him work, but she failed miserably.

He moved with precision, testing the shelf's stability, examining the brackets, and making minor adjustments that suggested he actually knew what he was doing. His hands were competent in a way that made her envy the shelving.

"Oliver!" A grandmother's voice called from the children's section. "Stop smelling the books and choose one."

"But they all smell different!" A small boy with wide eyes appeared around the corner, dragging his patient grandmother behind him.

Carrie blinked. The boy was holding a book she recognized. "Is that from the window display?"

"*Great Expectations*, Easy Classics Edition," the grandmother said apologetically. "He liked the cover."

"His hat's cool," Oliver announced, pointing at Pip on the cover.

"Solid reasoning," Tanner said without looking up from the shelf. He paused until Oliver was gone, then he reached for the full Penguin Classics edition on a nearby shelf and flipped through the pages like he was looking for a specific passage.

He ran his finger down the page and found it.

Then, as if compelled by something beyond his control, he read aloud, "I loved her against reason, against promise, against peace, against hope, against happiness, against all discouragement that could be."

The shop went silent. Even the ancient heating system stopped its wheezing to listen.

He'd just read Carrie's chapter twenty-nine line, the one that made her forget how to breathe. And he'd read it like it was nothing, like her entire nervous system hadn't erupted in volcanic desire, spreading like a molten puddle all over the floor.

Tanner looked up, seemed to realize what he'd done, and cleared his throat. "Good line," he said. "I doubt it's in Oliver's version, though. So he'll grow up thinking that he knows the story without ever knowing the language and writing that made it a classic in the first place."

Carrie was still processing not only the thought but that it came from him—from *The Voice*, the voice that had just read *The Line*—when he turned back to his work.

"You okay?" Shannon whispered, appearing at Carrie's elbow.

"I'm totally fine. Completely normal."

"You just alphabetized the sugar packets."

Carrie looked down. She had, in fact, arranged the coffee station's sugar and creamer packets alphabetically by brand name. "It's more efficient."

"Than color? It's just yellow, pink, brown, and white." Shannon studied her face. "Do you need to sit down?"

"I need to work."

But working was difficult when Tanner Blake was fifteen feet away, fixing her shelf with those massively capable hands while her brain played chapter twenty-nine on a loop.

He finished half an hour later, testing the shelf's

stability with his full weight. "That'll hold. But the footer's a temporary fix. You should have the whole unit reanchored to the wall. I can do it tomorrow if you want."

"I can't afford you." The words were out before Carrie could stop them.

He started packing his tools. "There's no charge. It's no problem. I'm your upstairs neighbor fixing a safety hazard." He closed the toolbox and headed for the back stairs, then paused. "For what it's worth—I appreciate you not making a big deal out of who I am. Most people either pretend they don't know or they can't stop knowing, if that makes sense."

"It makes sense."

He nodded and left, footsteps fading upstairs.

Shannon waited exactly three seconds. "Oh, my gosh!"

"I know."

"He's gorgeous, talented, and he fixes things."

"So I noticed."

Shannon was still staring at the stairs. "You're going to fall for him so hard."

"I'm not going to fall for anyone. I'm going to save this shop, prove Dennis wrong, and learn to run a business that doesn't hemorrhage money." Carrie grabbed her marker and fresh index cards. "Now help me hang the Secret Santa letters. It's tradition."

She wrote on the first card in her neatest print:

> *Tell us your Christmas wish.*
> *Your friends at Lamplight Books*

They'd done Secret Santa letters for three years now—anonymous wishes clipped to twine in the window, little gifts appearing like magic when someone in town could grant them. Those who didn't take part still came to read the letters, their faces soft with remembered wonder.

This year had to be different. This year had to save her.

Carrie clipped the card to the twine and tried to ignore the way her hands shook just a little as she twisted the pine garland around the doorframe.

Inside, the morning routine continued. She sold the Dickens to Oliver's grandmother, recommended a cookbook to someone who "didn't really cook but wanted to start," and wrapped books in paper that made the packages look special.

The shop was charming and discouragingly quiet.

By noon, she'd made forty-seven dollars.

That afternoon, Carrie tried not to listen to chapter twenty-nine again. She tried not to think about the way Tanner's thumb had brushed her palm or how his voice reading Dickens had made her knees forget what they were there for. And she remembered how his voice sounded saying her name.

Tanner closed the apartment door and leaned against it, toolbox still in hand.

Safe.

The word felt foreign. He'd been running for three weeks, and this was the first place that felt like a place he could rest instead of hide.

He set the toolbox down and pulled out his phone. Forty-seven unread messages, each one a small demand

on the person he used to be. His agent wanted a statement. His publicist had crafted apologies he needed to
approve. Journalists who'd been friendly last month
were now asking if he had anger issues. And buried
among them were messages from people he'd thought
were friends, asking if the rumors were true or
suggesting he might need some "help."

He'd watched his career dismantle itself in real time
over the past several days. Not the dramatic explosion
he'd feared, but a slow erosion. Recording sessions were
"postponed." Meetings were "rescheduled" with the
polite distance of an industry deciding whether he was
worth the risk.

The Google Alert notification sat at the top of his
screen, the number climbing even as he watched.
"Tanner Blake"—247 new results.

He set his phone on the counter without opening
any of it. He'd read enough versions to know what they
would say. The headline was always some variation of
"Bad Santa," the comments always the same mix of
outrage and schadenfreude, and the think pieces always
questioning his character, his professionalism, and his
future.

What none of them mentioned was the hospital.
The children who'd been counting on that fundraiser.
The hundred thousand dollars in lost funding because
of fifteen seconds of video that didn't show the hours of
psychological warfare that preceded it.

That was the only part that mattered.

But he had escaped, for the moment. The apartment was small and furnished, but barely. Mrs.
Snyder had apologized for its condition when she'd
shown it to him yesterday. "The last tenant left in a

hurry," she'd said. "But it's quiet, and no one will bother you here."

Quiet. That was what he needed.

He walked to the window and looked down at Main Street. Snow was falling and catching the light from the old-fashioned streetlamps. Hollydale looked like a postcard of the kind of town that still believed in things like community, kindness, and second chances.

The kind of town he'd inadvertently hurt.

He'd come to Hollydale deliberately, not to hide from what he'd done, but to face it. The hospital was six blocks away. He could see it from his bedroom window. Every morning, he would wake up and see the building where children were missing out on their much-needed funding because of him.

Some people might call that masochistic. He called it accountability.

The floorboards creaked beneath him. Below, he could hear voices. The woman with the green glasses—Shannon—was talking, her voice carrying through the old building's floorboards. He couldn't make out the words, just her tone—excitement, disbelief.

Then Carrie's voice, quieter, steadier.

Carrie Watson. The woman who'd recognized him instantly and then, of all things, let him be invisible.

He'd been braced for the usual reaction—the squealing, the demands for photos, and the invasive questions about the scandal. Or worse, the cold shoulder, the judgment, and the assumption that he was exactly what the internet said he was.

Instead, she'd looked at him and seen someone who needed safe harbor. And she gave it to him.

He pulled off his beanie and ran his hand through

his hair. The apartment was cold. He turned up the heat and, on the way to finish unpacking, caught sight of the small pile of recording equipment. At some point, he would need to do something about the wreckage of his career. Not today.

Instead, he stood at the window and watched the snow fall on a town that had every reason to hate him.

His phone buzzed. The screen lit up with his agent's name, then his publicist's, then a number he didn't recognize—probably another journalist. He watched the notifications pile up, each one a reminder of the career that had defined him for five years—the careful statements, the strategic appearances, the version of himself that existed only for cameras and microphones.

For once, he let them all go unanswered.

Tomorrow, he would go back downstairs. He would offer to fix something else. The reading chair looked wobbly. The coffee station's cart had a loose wheel. Small things. Useful things. Things that had nothing to do with fame or scandal or the person the world thought he was. Things that might, in some small way, distract him from what he'd cost this town.

He thought about Carrie's face when she'd realized who he was. The flash of recognition, then something else. Not judgment. Understanding, maybe. She'd looked at him the way he imagined she looked at broken books that just needed the right kind of care.

Nice to meet you, Tom.

Tom, not Tanner Blake, the celebrity. Not Tanner Blake, the scandal. Just Tom, the guy upstairs with a toolbox.

He could be that person. He wanted to be that person.

The voices downstairs faded. A door closed. The shop went quiet.

Tanner turned away from the window and started unpacking.

Tomorrow, he would be Tom and fix something else while he tried to earn the second chance Carrie had given him without even knowing she had.

For tonight, he was grateful to be somewhere he could breathe.

CHAPTER TWO

THE NEXT MORNING brought Tanner with coffee and a question.

"The reading chair," he said, setting a cup on the counter. "It's wobbly. Mind if I take a look?"

Carrie stared at the coffee. It was from the place two blocks over, the one she'd stopped going to when she tightened her budget. "You brought me coffee."

"You looked like you needed it yesterday. Black, right? I guessed."

"You guessed right." She took the cup, and their fingers brushed. Again. This was becoming a problem. "The chair by the window? You really don't have to—"

"I know I don't have to." He was already grabbing the chair and heading toward the back of the shop.

He set the chair down in the small back room, testing the legs. The space was cramped—desk over-flowing with paperwork, inventory boxes stacked against one wall, a whiteboard covered in Post-it notes and reminders. It was an organized mess, the kind that came from someone working too hard with not enough help.

His eyes caught a document at the top of the desk pile. He didn't mean to read it, but the bold red letters were impossible to ignore:

LEASE RENEWAL NOTICE - PAYMENT DUE DECEMBER 27.

And below that, the amount: $5,000.00.

Five thousand dollars or the space reverted to the landlord.

He looked away quickly and focused on the chair. It was none of his business. She'd made it clear she didn't want help. She didn't want to be rescued. The last thing she needed was his prying into her finances, but the number stuck in his head.

SHANNON APPEARED beside Carrie the moment he was out of earshot. "He brought you coffee."

"I noticed."

"Expensive coffee."

"Also noticed."

"From that place we love."

"Shannon—"

Shannon furrowed her eyebrows. "I like coffee. I must not look like I need it." She added, "Note to self: stop looking awake." She gave Carrie a knowing look. "So, this is happening."

"Nothing's happening. He's being nice. He probably feels sorry for me because of the shelf thing."

"The shelf thing where he saved your life, and you stapled him?" She smiled as she scrolled through her phone.

"His sleeve. I stapled his sleeve." Carrie stopped.

"Oh!" Shannon's expression shifted from glee to concern. "There's some news here about your staple gun guy."

"He's not my—" Carrie rolled her eyes. "What news?"

Shannon turned her phone around. A blog post filled the screen, headlined in festive red and green.

EXCLUSIVE: 'Bad Santa' Tanner Blake Hiding in Small Town After Scandal Costs Hospital Fundraiser

Carrie's stomach dropped, and the words blurred together as she read, "After a viral talk show incident, Hollydale Children's Hospital loses a hundred thousand in funding when publishers pull actor Tanner Blake's live book reading event from their Christmas fundraiser."

"A hundred thousand dollars?" Carrie read it again.

"He cost them their fundraiser," Shannon whispered. "The hospital's pediatric wing. Children who need surgeries, treatments."

Carrie sank onto the counter stool, still reading. The article was brief but brutal—screenshots from social media, people calling him names, demanding apologies. His career was crumbling in real time. She handed the phone back to Shannon and tried to absorb it.

"Oh, there's more," Shannon said, scrolling. "The real video—the full, unedited one from the talk show—is buried, but I found a copy. Diamonds and the internet are forever."

Carrie watched as the host, guest Portia Pembroke, and her beloved voice actor took their seats after a holiday skit. They were still wearing their Santa hats as Tanner explained his latest project. He gestured broadly and accidentally splashed his mug of water on Portia Pembroke, seated beside him.

After a dramatic gasp, she narrowed her eyes and snapped, "You stupid idiot! This dress is worth more than your mother's trailer!"

Tanner, stunned for a second, soon rallied. "Oh, I don't doubt its worth because that dress has more brains and talent in its zipper tab than the person wearing it—you shallow, mean-spirited shrew!"

Portia Pembroke blinked in disbelief before unleashing a string of vitriol ending with: "You really think you're the star here? You're lucky you've made it this far in the industry, but don't expect to get farther. You're done." She turned to someone off-camera and commanded, "Fix that in post."

The host hastily chimed in, "We'll be right back after a word from our sponsors."

Carrie said, "Well, everyone knows she's a horrible person. She's on all those lists of mean celebrities."

Shannon slipped her phone back into her pocket. "Yeah, but the viral version just shows him unloading on her, so he looks like a big bully attacking a vulnerable woman."

"That's character assassination," Carrie said.

"That's the internet." Shannon took her phone back. "But that hospital still lost its funding. Those children still need medical treatment. And he's over there fixing our reading chair like nothing happened."

Carrie glanced toward the back room, and the steady sound of tools being set down, the creak of wood, and the quiet competence of someone who knew how to fix broken things drifted out. "So that's why he's here and asked me to call him Tom. He's trying to hide from the scandal."

"Can you blame him?"

"No, not at all." Carrie stood.

Shannon nodded and rested her chin on her hands.

Carrie leaned on her elbow and thought for a moment. "But why would he come here where the hospital is? I mean, wouldn't he want to be anywhere but here?"

"Good point. He's fresh in everyone's mind since the scandal, and not in a good way." Shannon gazed abstractedly at the front window. "But isn't he really known more for his voice? I mean, I know he's an actor, but he's one of those actors that nobody recognizes, you know?"

"I doubt he would like hearing it put quite that way." Carrie glanced toward the back where Tanner was working.

Shannon shrugged. "Sorry, but it is what it is."

Carrie couldn't argue the point. "But I still don't get it. He's obviously hiding, but why here?"

Shannon looked around the store. "Maybe because, judging from our customer traffic, we're practically invisible?" She let out a weak laugh. "He's desperate to hide, and we're desperate for people to notice we're here. It's kind of funny, but not really."

Carrie looked through the display window toward the hospital. An idea was forming, still nebulous but growing clearer. "Shannon, what if we could fix both problems?"

"What are you thinking?"

"I'm thinking of our Secret Santa tradition. People love that sort of thing. Anonymous gifts. Acts of kindness." Carrie pulled out her phone and started searching. "I mean, we've never done a charity event, but what if we did? What if we did something for the hospital?"

"Like what?"

"I don't know. Maybe take our Secret Santa tradition to the children. Oh! Or we could donate books for people to read to the children. They could get sponsors, and the proceeds would go to the hospital. I don't know. It's an idea. I just think there must be something we could do."

"'A hundred thousand dollars' worth of something? That's a lot of reading." Shannon had the same look on her face that she got when Carrie came up with impossible display window ideas.

"Maybe not a hundred thousand, but we could raise some money. It would help the children, and it would give us free publicity. Everyone wins."

"And Tanner?"

"Doesn't need to be involved. He's just the guy upstairs with a tool belt. Who knows? This might even take the spotlight off his situation."

Shannon studied her. "You're trying to protect him."

"I'm trying to help children and save our shop. If that also happens to take some pressure off a guy who got screwed by social media, then good."

Over the next few days, the idea took shape. Carrie reached out to the hospital and proposed a partnership: "Christmas Stories by Lamplight Books." Local volunteers would visit the pediatric wing to read to the children in person, with sponsors backing each reader. The children could write Secret Santa letters with their wishes—kept anonymous to protect privacy—and the hospital could share a general wish list on their blog. Community members could sign up to fulfill specific wishes. The event would culminate on December 22 with an evening story hour at the hospital, where Santa would read to all the children by lamplight and pass out the presents the children had wished for.

The hospital loved it. The local paper loved it. The story got picked up by the regional news.

What Carrie hadn't expected was the feedback.

The messages started arriving as soon as the webpage went live. People wanted to help. The nurses made it a project, giving the children special paper and envelopes decorated with snowflakes and reindeer. Before they hung the real letters to Santa with clothespins and twine at the hospital, Shannon scanned them and posted them online so people could sign up to contribute.

"Dear Santa," wrote a seven-year-old named Hailey with careful, looping letters. "I wish I could go home and see my dog, Biscuit, on Christmas morning. He doesn't understand why I'm gone. When you see him, can you tell him I miss him?"

"Dear Santa," wrote a ten-year-old named Marco. "I

wish my little sister could visit me. She's too young to be in the hospital, but I miss her. Can you make her older just for one day?"

"Dear Santa," wrote a five-year-old named Jade. "I wish the snow would come inside so I could touch it. I've been here since September, and I forgot what snow feels like."

Carrie read them in the back room and had to sit down. Shannon found her there, letters spread across the desk, eyes damp.

"Shannon, these kids just want normal things—to see their pets, their siblings, and snow. And we're selling books."

"We're raising money for their care. That's not nothing."

"But we could do more. We could—" Carrie looked at the letters again. "Not just deliver gifts but have Santa answer their letters during the event. It would make it more about them in a tangible sense. They don't understand fundraising, but they'll understand Santa."

"Where are you going to find Santa on three days' notice at this time of year?"

Carrie was already thinking about the man upstairs, the one with the voice that made people listen, the one who was hiding from the world. But maybe he would consider it if he could give some sick children some Christmas magic.

"I have an idea," she said. "But you're going to think I'm crazy."

"Going to? No, I already think that. What's the idea?"

"Tanner," Carrie said. "We need Tanner to be Santa."

Shannon's face registered something between laughter and horror. "Tanner? Bad Santa?"

TANNER LAY on the couch in his apartment, staring at the ceiling and listening to the old building settle around him.

Eight forty-three p.m., too early to sleep but too late to do anything productive.

Below, the bookshop was quiet. Carrie had left an hour ago, and he'd watched from his window as she'd walked to her car, shoulders hunched against the December cold. She'd paused at the driver's door and looked back at the shop as if she were memorizing it.

Or saying goodbye to it. He couldn't unsee the late rent notice on her desk. With her lease deadline days away, she might be facing closure.

He rolled onto his side and looked at his phone. The Secret Santa article was still open in his browser. Carrie had started the tradition three years ago. With its anonymous wishes and anonymous gifts, it was magic for people who'd stopped believing in it.

She'd built something beautiful in this shop. Anyone could see that: the carefully sections, the reading corner he'd fixed, the warm atmosphere that made people want to curl up with a book. She'd taken the shell of a store space and turned it into a place that mattered.

And it still wasn't enough.

He could write a check right now, put it in a Secret Santa envelope, and slide it under her door. Five thousand dollars—problem solved. But she would know it was from him. And then what? She would think he pitied her. Or worse, that he thought she couldn't handle her own problems.

She'd mentioned her ex—Dennis—more than once, with bitterness in her voice. She'd left someone who'd had no faith in her, and she was determined to prove him wrong. She was building something on her own terms, refusing shortcuts even when they might save her.

He understood that.

He'd spent five years taking whatever roles his agent pitched, doing whatever his publicist suggested, being whoever they said he should be. But the longer he spent in the business, the less he believed he belonged there. He loved acting, but that was such a small part of his work. Most of it involved people whose values he frankly didn't care for. The whole Portia incident merely brought it to the surface—not that he'd handled that well.

Maybe that was why he felt such a kinship with Carrie. Despite being in different spheres, they both wanted the same thing—to be more than what someone else said they were.

A floorboard creaked somewhere in the apartment. The radiator hissed and clanked, doing its best to fight off the December cold.

He recalled bringing her morning coffee and the surprise on her face, as if small kindnesses were foreign to her. He wished he could do more. The wobbly chair didn't count; it was an easy fix—twenty minutes at most. He had nothing but time, and she had enough to worry about. But giving her rent money would be too much to offer; she would never accept it. So tomorrow, he would fix her back door that was sticking. It was one more thing he could make right before he left.

Because he would leave.

He gazed out the window where snow was beginning to fall again. Somewhere in this mess of scandal and struggle, he would find a way forward.

He had to.

CHAPTER THREE

TANNER WAS REWIRING the lamp in the fiction section when Carrie found him.

"I need to ask you something," she said. "And you can say no. Absolutely, completely, no-hard-feelings no."

He looked up from the collection of lamp parts, eyebrows raised. "That's a concerning preamble."

"We're doing a charity event for the Hollydale Children's Hospital. Community members are reading to children to raise money for their pediatric wing."

"Yeah, I've seen the flyers."

"I know about the fundraiser you were supposed to do. I know what happened. And this isn't about that."

He set down the wire strippers and looked at her with dread in his eyes.

"Our Santa just canceled this morning. Stomach flu." She pulled copies of the letters from her pocket. "The thing is, we have these letters from the children at the hospital. They wrote to Santa with their wishes and hopes. Santa was going to answer their letters during the event tomorrow. Only we don't have a Santa, so . . ."

"So you thought they would love to have the guy who cost them a hundred grand dress up and play Santa?" His voice was flat.

"I thought the guy who loves children and does charity work might want to help make their Christmas special. It's a lot to ask, so I'll understand if you can't. But the children . . . And no one has to know that it's you." She waited. "Please?"

He took the letters, read Hailey's wish about her dog, Marco's about his sister, and Jade's about the snow.

His jaw worked. When he looked up, his eyes were bright. "Nobody would know it's me?"

"Full costume. Beard, suit, the works. You'd just be Santa, anonymous and safe."

"What about my voice? People recognize—"

"It's possible, but in that context, what are the odds of anyone making that connection?" She stopped. "But I'm not going to lie. It's a risk. But the children need to know their Christmas wishes matter."

He read the letters again, slower this time, like he was memorizing every word.

"I've been doing charity events since I was in high school," he said finally. "Children's hospitals, literacy programs, library fundraisers. I love doing it. But that one stupid video—" He stopped. "But . . . I've ruined Christmas, so I owe it to those children."

"You don't owe them."

"Yes, I do." He handed the letters back. "When is it?"

"Tomorrow. Seven p.m."

"Okay. I'll be Santa."

"Thank you!" She fought the urge to throw her arms around his neck and hug him. Her heart swelled with affection for this man who was about to face a difficult situation but was willing to do it for the children.

Before she could stop herself, Carrie said, "For what it's worth, you didn't ruin Christmas. You had one bad moment on national television. That doesn't erase all the good you've done."

"Tell that to the internet."

"The internet is full of people who've forgotten that they make mistakes and love judging those who have." She met his eyes. "I'm not one of them."

His expression shifted, as if he had something important to say. Instead, he just nodded. "Seven p.m. I'll be ready."

THE SANTA SUIT lay across his bed like a red velvet accusation. Tanner picked up the jacket, heavier than he'd expected. The fabric was worn at the elbows, shiny in places from years of use. How many other men had worn this? How many other Christmas Eves had it seen?

Tanner unfolded the letters again and gazed at Hailey's careful handwriting, Marco's smudged pencil, and Jade's crayon drawings in the margins. These children didn't know who Tanner Blake was. They definitely didn't know about the scandal or the lost funding. They just wanted someone to tell them Christmas still happened when they were stuck in hospital beds.

He'd done dozens of hospital readings over the years. It started by chance. A friend's child was sick, so he went to visit with a book that he thought she would enjoy, and somehow it became his thing. It made his rollercoaster of a career feel worthwhile. He never wanted to be famous. He wanted to tell stories. The hospital visits let him do that in their purest form.

Until Portia ruined it.

No, that wasn't fair. He did it to himself. He lost his temper and gave her exactly what she'd been angling for. She'd been difficult all day, making demands, needling him, and making snide comments about how lucky he was to be on a show with her. He'd held it together until she made that crack about his mother. He should have known better.

The suit's beard smelled like dust. He held it up to his face and looked in the mirror. Ridiculous. He looked like a mall Santa who'd lost his job and kept the uniform. But the children would see Santa. That was the magic of being young enough—you saw what you needed to see.

He thought about Carrie downstairs, probably going over her notes for the twentieth time. She'd created this entire event in three days, convinced the hospital to partner, gotten the word out online, and rallied the local community—all while her own business was failing.

Shannon had mentioned business troubles while Carrie was in the back room, so he admitted he'd seen the rent notice. He hoped his assumption was wrong, but Shannon confirmed it. Lamplight Books would probably close before the year was out. But Carrie hadn't said a word to him about it. She was apparently too proud to ask for help.

He respected that, and he understood it. He'd

grown up watching his mother work two jobs rather than ask his father for child support. Pride could be expensive, but sometimes it was all you had.

The Santa pants were too short, but he hoped his black boots would hide it. The hat barely stretched over his head. The whole look fell short of the magical Santa these children needed, but it was all he had, so he would make it work somehow.

His laptop chimed with an email from his audiobook publisher. They were reconsidering his contract for the upcoming spring recording schedule. It was industry speak for waiting to see if he was still toxic.

Tomorrow would determine that. If the fundraiser went well, it might shift the narrative away from him. But it was crucial that he kept his identity hidden, or he would make his PR nightmare even worse.

The smarter choice would have been to say no. But when Carrie held out those letters, she hadn't begged, demanded, or guilted him into it. She'd just offered him a chance to be useful again—to use his voice for something that mattered.

He folded the suit carefully and placed it on the chair by the window. Through the glass, he could see Main Street preparing for tomorrow: families hanging lights, the diner extending its hours, and the whole town gearing up to support the children.

And Carrie's bookshop stood at the center of it all.

Right now, sitting in his drafty apartment above a failing bookshop, he was glad to be part of it all. It gave him a purpose—to get through tomorrow, make children smile, and then go home to LA and try to salvage his career.

He would try not to think about what he would be leaving.

THE NEXT DAY blurred into frenzied preparations. Shannon handled logistics while Carrie set up the reading corner, tested the video equipment, and arranged the special edition books and the small stack of letters. The local news confirmed they would send a reporter, and a local podcaster was going to livestream the event.

At six-thirty, the event space began filling up with family members, while others watched the livestream from the bookstore. Parents brought their children, and elderly couples attended who remembered when downtown Hollydale's main street was thriving. Teenagers who'd heard about the event on social media were there, and Mrs. Snyder arrived with her bridge club.

At six forty-five, there was no Santa in sight.

"Where is he?" Shannon hissed. "Carrie, if he bailed—"

In the doorway, a figure in full Santa regalia appeared—red suit, white beard, black boots, the works. Only the eyes were visible, dark and familiar beneath the white eyebrows and red hat.

"Ho ho ho," Tanner said dryly. "Are you sure they won't recognize me?"

"You look perfect." Carrie adjusted his beard. "Can you breathe?"

"Barely."

"More importantly, can you read?"

"We're about to find out."

At seven p.m., Carrie welcomed everyone, explained the partnership with the hospital, and introduced the special books they'd donated. Then she brought out Santa.

The children in the crowd gasped with delight. The adults smiled. Tanner/Tom/Santa settled into the reading chair he'd fixed just days ago, and Carrie handed him the first letter.

"This is from Hailey," he said, searching the group of children before him. She raised her hand, and he smiled.

"Dear Santa," Tanner read, his voice warm and steady through the beard. "I wish I could go home and see my dog, Biscuit, on Christmas morning. He doesn't understand why I'm gone. Can you tell him I miss him?"

The room went quiet. Tanner looked at Hailey.

"Well, Hailey," he said. "I had a talk with Biscuit just the other day—Santa has special ways of talking to dogs, you know. He told me he misses you too, but he wants you to know he understands you're getting better. Dogs are smart that way. They know that sometimes people have to be away so they can come back stronger. He's waiting for you and keeping your spot on the couch warm for when you get home."

A beaming Hailey clapped.

Tanner's shoulders relaxed a fraction. He reached for the next letter.

"This is from Marco." Marco raised his hand. He read the wish about Marco's sister being old enough to visit. "Marco, I checked with the North Pole rules department. Oh yes, we have rules that apply only at Christmas. And I pulled some strings." A woman, clearly Marco's mother, led a young girl to Marco's wheelchair, and they hugged.

After a few moments passed and a few eyes were wiped, Santa said, "The best presents aren't always the ones under the tree. Sometimes they're the ones that show up when you need them most."

Marco smiled through his tears.

Then came Jade's letter—the one about snow.

Tanner read it slowly. When he finished, he was quiet. Then:

"Dear Jade, snow is patient. It waits for the perfect moment, and then it falls when you least expect it. I can't bring it inside the hospital, but I can promise you this: when you see it again, it'll be even more beautiful than you remembered. Until then, close your eyes and imagine it. Remember that each snowflake is different, just like you. So that means you're already carrying a little bit of winter magic inside you."

The reporter from the local news took photos while the podcaster filmed. Parents dabbed their eyes, while Mrs. Snyder, eyes streaming, pulled several tissues from her purse.

And then Tanner did an unexpected thing. He pulled out a book from beside his chair—not one they'd planned, but a worn copy of *A Christmas Carol* from the shop's classics section—and he read.

"Marley was dead, to begin with. There is no doubt whatever about that."

His voice filled the room, the same voice Carrie had been swooning over for months, but it was different in person, warmer and more real.

The children in the hospital watched, transfixed. The crowd grew still. Even Shannon, who'd been manning the donations table, had abandoned her post to listen.

As he read, a murmur rippled through the crowd. People leaned toward each other, whispering. Recognition dawning. That voice. That familiar, unmistakable voice.

Tanner kept reading, but his hands tightened on the book. He had to be hearing the murmurs of people realizing who he was.

Then a small child who looked about four years old walked up to Santa, fearless and curious, in the midst of his reading.

"You're too thin for Santa," the child announced.

Tanner paused. "I've been eating my vegetables."

"Can I see your beard?"

"Oh, I don't think—"

But the child was already reaching up, tiny fingers grasping the white synthetic hair and tugging.

The beard came away in the child's hand.

Tanner Blake's face was suddenly bare for everyone to see.

CHAPTER FOUR

THE ROOM WENT SILENT. Then the whispers started
in earnest.

"That's—"

"It's him."

"Tanner Blake."

"Bad Santa."

Hailey called out with delight, "You're the story
man! The one who was supposed to read to us before!
My mom showed me your picture."

Tanner sat frozen, the copy of Dickens still in his
hands, his cover blown. He looked at Carrie—panic
flashed in his eyes. The same panic from when she'd
first recognized him in the shop.

Then something changed. Maybe it was Hailey's
recognition. Maybe it was the fact that he'd already
read the letters, already given the children what they
needed. Maybe it was exhaustion from hiding.

He stood, set down the book, and looked directly at
the podcaster's phone lens.

"Yeah," he said. "I'm Tanner Blake. And I'm sorry.

I'm sorry the hospital lost their funding because of me. I'm sorry children nearly missed out on their Christmas story because I lost my temper on national television. I'm sorry I've let you down." He paused. "But I'm here now. And if you'll have me, I'd like to finish the story."

The room stayed silent. The reporter's camera, the podcaster's phone, and a growing number of other phones were trained on him. This was it—the moment that would define whether his career recovered or died completely.

Hailey asked, "Will you do the voices? The scary ghost voices?"

Tanner's laugh was surprised and genuine. "Yeah. I'll do the voices."

He picked up the book and kept reading. He did every voice—Scrooge, the ghosts, Tiny Tim. The children laughed, gasped, and smiled until Scrooge's Christmas morning redemption.

When he finished, the crowd applauded. The hospital children cheered. And the reporter dabbed her eye.

Mrs. Snyder stood up. "Young man, how much was that lost fundraiser? A hundred thousand?"

Tanner nodded warily.

"Well." She pulled out her checkbook. "I'm putting in a thousand. Who else?"

Oliver's grandmother rose from her seat in the back, while Oliver clutched his new copy of *Great Expectations*. "Three years ago, Oliver had leukemia. The pediatric wing saved his life. We can never repay what they did, but we can help other families. Here's ten thousand."

The crowd went silent. Ten thousand dollars. From one family.

Richard Walsh, whose law office had anchored Main Street for twenty years, stood. "Walsh & Partners will donate five thousand. Consider it an investment in our community."

And just like that, the crowd came alive. People pulled out wallets, wrote checks, and promised donations. Parents donated what they could. Mrs. Snyder's bridge club friends each wrote checks for five hundred. Teenagers Venmoed from their phones.

As the video spread online—Tanner Blake unmasked, apologizing, reading to sick children—donations started flooding into their GoFundMe website. They came from all over—people watching the livestream, former Hollydale residents who'd moved away, and people from neighboring towns who'd heard the story. And then there were the comments on the livestream, which were overwhelmingly supportive.

This is redemption done right.

He's actually doing something.

Within two hours, they'd raised eighteen thousand dollars in immediate donations, with another ten thousand in pledges over the next six months. As the last of the event guests filtered through the exits, Shannon ran the numbers three times on her phone. "We're two thousand short of our goal."

"I've got it." Tanner pulled out his phone and made a transfer right there. "That's the hospital fundraiser covered."

The reporter caught it all: the unmasking, the reading, the spontaneous fundraising, and Tanner's donation. She did a quick interview with him. "How does it feel to turn your Christmas around?"

He smiled, tired but sincere. "Charity is the best Christmas gift anyone could ask for."

The reporter left with her footage and a promise to run the story on the morning news.

By nine-thirty, Carrie, Shannon, and Tanner returned to the shop.

"Tanner, you did it," Carrie said. "You saved their fundraiser."

"You did it," he said. "This was all your event."

"You're the one who put your career on the line."

"My career was already on the line." He ran a hand through his hair. "At least now the children won't pay the price."

Shannon's phone buzzed. She looked at it, eyes widening. "Oh my gosh! Carrie. Look."

She held out her phone. A new video was already trending with the full story. Tanner unmasked, apologizing, finishing the reading, and donating his own money. The headline: "Bad Santa Becomes Real Santa: Tanner Blake Redeems Himself at Small Town Charity Event."

Comments were pouring in:

> This is what real apologies look like.

> He didn't have to do this, but he did anyway.

The way he talked to those children . . .
that's the real him.

The original, uncut video was surfacing. The truth was getting out.

Tanner's phone started ringing. He looked at the screen and went pale. "It's my agent."

He stepped outside to take it. Carrie and Shannon watched through the window as he paced, talked, and listened.

When he came back in, his expression was unreadable.

"I've got a potential film offer," he said. "They want me in LA in four days for a meeting."

"That's amazing!" Shannon said. "Right? That's amazing?"

"Yeah. It's amazing." But he was looking at Carrie. "It's everything I've been working toward. The kind of role that could change everything."

Shannon looked from Tanner to Carrie, then said softly, "Uh, I've got . . . stuff to do in the back room," and she disappeared.

"That's amazing." Carrie tried to sound excited, but her heart wasn't in it. She managed to keep her voice steady. "Tanner, this is your shot. You have to take it."

"I know." He reached into his pocket and pulled out a wrapped box. "But first—I found this. From Santa. It has your name on it."

Carrie took the box, recognizing the Secret Santa wrapping paper they'd used for the children's gifts. Inside was a folded check and a note: "For Carrie Watson, who gave children Christmas magic. From your Secret Santa."

The amount was exactly what she needed for her lease payment.

She looked up at Tanner, her eyes stinging. "Secret Santa's bank account had your name on it."

"I didn't have it in cash." But his eyes gave him away.

"But this is for five thousand dollars. I don't understand."

"I didn't mean to, but I happened to see the late due notice on your desk. You deserve a Christmas miracle as much as those children."

"Tanner, I can't accept this."

"It's not from me. It's from Santa, and I've got the suit to prove it."

Her phone buzzed in her pocket. She pulled it out and looked. "Dennis?"

> Rumor has it the bookshop is closing.
> I'm sorry to hear it, but I tried to warn
> you. Give me a call. I miss you. -D

Dennis. Somehow he'd found out. Of course he had. And now he thought she would come crawling back.

She looked at the check in her hand, then at Tanner. He was so kind to want to rescue her. And then she thought of Dennis. How like him to reach out when he knew she was down, thinking he could manipulate his way back into her life.

"Tanner, I can't take your money. I left Dennis to prove I could do this on my own, and I meant it. Succeed or fail, I've got to do it myself. Otherwise, I'd be trading one man's control for another man's rescue."

"Carrie, I didn't mean it like that—"

"I know. This is a kind and generous gift, because that's who you are. You've fixed all the things that were broken, and you've brought me coffee. And I love that about you. I love . . . that you want to save my shop. But I can't. How is succeeding with your help any different from Dennis telling me I'll fail without him?

"Because I believe you can succeed. This is just—"

"Me needing to be saved." She pressed the check into his hand. "And maybe you're right. But I have to figure it out on my own or at least try."

He looked at the check, then at her. "The payment's due in four days."

"I know." Her voice cracked slightly. "But I'd rather lose the shop than lose myself again." She smiled, and it almost felt real. "Go to LA. Take the role. Be amazing. I'll be here cheering you on from a distance."

He seemed ready to argue. Instead, he just nodded and pocketed the check. "Okay."

Carrie forced a smile, but when she lifted her eyes to meet his, she couldn't hide her conflicting emotions, her feelings about losing him to LA, and the knowledge that she had just sealed her fate.

His eyes darkened as he gazed intensely. "I'm not leaving yet. I need to know you're okay before I go." He gave her shoulder a squeeze and then headed for the stairs. At the doorway, he paused as if he had something to say, but he gave the door frame a pat and headed upstairs.

Minutes later, Shannon left, giving Carrie a hug on the way out. "Get some rest. It's been a long day."

But Carrie couldn't leave. Not yet.

The shop was quiet, just Carrie, the books, and the light from the streetlamps filtering through the window.

She walked slowly through the aisles, running her fingers along the spines: Fiction, Mystery, Romance, Children's books, Local authors. Each section she'd curated, organized, and loved into being.

She stopped at the shelf Tanner had fixed. She tested its stability the way he had, pressing her full weight against it. Solid. Dependable. Everything he was and what she tried to be.

The reading chair sat in the corner, no longer wobbly. She sank into it and pulled her knees to her chest. She could have saved it. The check was for exactly what she needed. Tanner had offered it freely, with no strings attached. Just take the money, pay the lease, and keep the doors open.

But that would have made Dennis right. You're not practical enough. Not business-minded. Too emotional. And worse: You'll always need someone to save you.

The Secret Santa letters hung in the window, wishes written by strangers—some fulfilled, some still waiting for magic. Her own wish—*Let me keep this place*—would go unanswered.

Carrie stood and walked to the counter, touching the vintage cash register she'd restored herself, the coffee station she'd built from a flea market cart, and the handwritten recommendation cards she'd spent hours creating. Every corner held a piece of her determination to succeed.

Three days. She had three days, and then it would be gone. Ahab Coffee would gut the space, install their corporate fixtures, and erase every trace of what she'd built. Before long, no one would remember Lamplight Books was ever here.

The tears came then, silent and steady. Not pretty

tears, but the ugly kind that poured out with the death of a dream. She'd done everything right—created beauty, served her community, helped sick children—and it still wasn't enough.

She considered calling the bank to beg for a loan. It wasn't too late to call Tanner and tell him that she'd changed her mind. All she had to do was let go of her principles.

But she couldn't. She wouldn't. If she was going to fail, she would fail as herself. Not as Dennis's ex or Tanner's charity case, but as Carrie Watson, who tried and fell short but never compromised who she was.

She turned off the lights one by one. The reading corner went dark. The children's section. The romance novels. Finally, just the lamp by the register was still glowing.

"I'm sorry," she whispered to the books, to the walls, to the dream that was dying. "I tried. I really tried."

She always left that one light on so the books wouldn't be lonely, and she locked the door behind her.

The drive home took twelve minutes. Twelve minutes of streetlights blurring past, of Christmas decorations mocking her failure, and of her phone sitting silent in the cup holder.

She'd lost. But at least she'd lost on her own terms.

CHAPTER FIVE

TANNER STOOD at his apartment window, looking down at the light from the single lamp Carrie had left burning in the bookshop. She'd been gone for twenty minutes, leaving light spilling onto the sidewalk.

His phone buzzed against the kitchen counter where he'd abandoned it. Fourteen missed calls from Sloane, his publicist. Twenty-three texts. He didn't need to read them to know what they said. The charity event story was everywhere now, which meant his location was blown.

He picked up the phone, thumb hovering over Sloane's contact. With one call, she could have a car here in three hours, spiriting him away to some other small town where nobody knew about the hospital children, or the lost funding, or Portia's perfectly edited victim performance.

The bookshop's light caught his eye again.

Nice to meet you, Tom. She'd known exactly who he was, but she'd offered him invisibility, anyway.

His phone rang. Sloane.

"Where the hell are you?" Her voice was sharp with professional panic. "Someone posted a photo from that bookshop event. You're trending again."

"I know."

"The Crescent Gate Studios meeting is in four days. If you're not back in LA—"

"I'll be there." He watched a cat cross Main Street below, unhurried. "But not yet."

"Tanner, that's insane. The longer you stay, the more likely—"

"The event raised thirty thousand for the hospital, and more keeps pouring in. The real story is getting traction. Portia's team is in damage control mode." He moved away from the window. "Things are turning around."

"Because you got lucky. Some small-town bookshop owner decided to let you play Santa. That doesn't mean you should—"

"Sloane, I'm staying."

Silence. Then she said, "This is about a woman, isn't it?"

Was it? The memory of Carrie's hand in his surfaced unbidden. Then he thought of the way she'd yanked out her earbud the first day he walked in. He wished she hadn't refused his check, but he loved the fierce pride that drove her to achieve on her own.

Maybe it was about a woman, but he wasn't about to admit it to Sloane. "It's about needing to be some-where real for five minutes."

Sloane sighed. "Don't do anything stupid. No more public appearances. No more Santa suits. And defi-nitely no more viral moments."

After she hung up, he pulled up the news coverage

on his laptop. There he was in the Santa suit, beard askew, surrounded by crying children and grateful parents. The comments were brutal in some places, supportive in others. The internet was doing what it did best—tearing people apart and building them up simultaneously.

But then he found a different video, shot on someone's phone. It showed the moment after the beard came off. Carrie stepping toward him, not away. Her hand touched his arm so briefly the camera almost missed it. In the face of the universal condemnation he expected, she'd been there with a gesture of support when he needed it most. It was what she did best. She simply cared in her own quiet way unconditionally, and he loved that about her.

He closed the laptop and looked around the apartment. It was nothing like his place in LA with its water-stained ceiling in one corner, radiator that clanged like the ghost of Marley in chains, and the windows that rattled when the wind blew down Main Street. But from here, he felt closer to life. Real life was happening all around him. Next door, the couple was having their usual post-dinner debate. Somewhere else, a dog barked. Outside, the faint sound of Christmas music from a passing car filtered in through his windows.

In LA, his apartment was soundproofed. It was perfect for recording and for isolation. He'd moved there after his career took off, when background noise became the enemy of clean audio. But somewhere along the way, the silence became more than a professional necessity. It was his personal default. He wished that would change.

For now, he felt alive and connected. Tomorrow, he

would fix more shelves and maybe help with the inventory. Most of all, he would pretend his entire future didn't hang on a meeting. But he couldn't hide from the fact that success would mean leaving a place where someone called him Tom around others.

Did Carrie know that she'd given him more than a nickname and privacy? She'd given him permission to feel normal and useful again. Life here wasn't just about him. He'd forgotten what it felt like to matter to others in a way that had nothing to do with fame or scandal or the cruel judgment of strangers online.

But soon he would leave it behind. The meeting was everything he'd worked toward. That kind of opportunity never came twice.

But for now, for these few days remaining, he could still be the guy from upstairs with a toolbox and time to help.

THE NEXT MORNING, the story was everywhere. "Bad Santa Redeems Himself" had gone viral in the best way. Tanner's donation, his reading, and the fundraising were all anyone could talk about. The bookshop's phone wouldn't stop ringing. People called ordering books. Others came shopping in person. Several asked when the next event would be.

Carrie should have been thrilled, but instead, she felt hollow. The event had been a massive success for the hospital and for Tanner's reputation. But her lease payment was due in four days, and despite the surge in interest and the resulting book sales, it wasn't enough.

The reporter from Channel 7 stopped by that afternoon. She'd been covering the event and had struck up a friendship with Carrie.

"How are you doing?" the reporter asked, setting down her coffee. "You look exhausted."

"I'm fine," Carrie said automatically, then stopped. "Actually, no. I'm not fine. The event was wonderful, and I'm so glad we helped those children, but . . ." She gestured at the beautiful, quiet shop. "This place is still going under. My lease payment is due on the 27th, and even with the publicity, I don't have it."

"But surely after everything you did for the hospital—"

"Tanner offered to help, but I couldn't take his money."

The reporter studied her with shrewd eyes. "You know, we're running a follow-up segment tonight. About the event's impact on the community. Mind if I mention the bookshop's situation? Sometimes people just need to know there's a need."

"I don't want charity—"

"It's not charity. It's community. You gave to them. Maybe they would like to give back."

That night, the segment aired. The reporter talked about the event's success, showed clips of Tanner reading to the children, and interviewed parents whose children had received Secret Santa gifts. She ended with, "Lamplight Books, the shop that organized this beautiful event, has been struggling to stay afloat. Owner Carrie Watson has poured her heart into creating a warm, welcoming space for our community, and now that community has a chance to give back. The shop's lease payment is due December 27th. Tomorrow is their last day open before Christmas Eve.

If you've been meaning to buy that last-minute Christmas gift, maybe consider shopping local. Books make great gifts."

December 23RD dawned cold and clear.

Carrie arrived at seven to open at eight and found a line already forming outside. Mrs. Snyder stood at the front, bundled in her winter coat.

"We saw the news," Mrs. Snyder said simply. "We're here to shop."

The day became a blur. A steady stream of people poured in throughout the day: neighbors she'd never met, parents from the hospital event, teachers from the elementary school, and the teenagers who usually hung out at the coffee shop. Oliver and his grandmother were back for more books.

By ten o'clock, Shannon had abandoned any pretense of her day off and was working a register. By noon, they'd run out of shopping bags and started using paper lunch sacks from the deli next door.

"I need help," Carrie called to Shannon. "Is your boyfriend free? Can he run a register?"

But before Shannon could answer, Tanner walked in. He'd slept in, but while sipping his coffee, he happened to glance out the window and saw the line. He came downstairs to make sure she was okay.

"Put me to work," he said, rolling up his sleeves.

So there they were, the three of them, racing between shelves and registers. Tanner hauled boxes from the back room to restock what they could. Shannon rang up sales and wrapped gifts. Carrie recommended books and found alternatives when her first suggestions were sold out. They all thanked each person who walked through the door.

The reporter stopped by at three, filmed the flurry of activity, and interviewed customers in line.

"What brought you here today?" she asked a young father.

"Christmas Eve. It's tomorrow, and no one should have to spend Christmas Eve closing a business. This is our town's only bookstore. It matters to us."

Not everyone bought much, but they bought what they could. Some could only afford a bookmark or a single paperback. But they came—five hundred people, maybe more, throughout the day. Ten dollars here, twenty there, and one woman bought two hundred dollars' worth of books for her book club's next two sessions.

At eight p.m., the last customer left, and Carrie flipped the sign to closed. She turned back and looked at the sparsely populated shelves, scattered cardboard boxes, and the coffee station long since drained.

The three of them sat behind the counter, too exhausted to stand.

"I can't feel my feet," Shannon said.

"I can't feel my face," Tanner added.

"I can't feel anything," Carrie said, then laughed. It was slightly hysterical. "How much did we make?"

Shannon counted the cash and then tallied the sales for the day. The total had been steadily climbing—ten dollars here, fifty there, the book club's two hundred, and the online sales had been coming in all day as well. They'd even received some online donations after the morning news segment aired.

Carrie looked over Shannon's shoulder at the computer screen and blinked. She leaned closer. "Is that real? Are you sure?"

A stunned Shannon stared at the screen. "Six thousand, eight hundred and forty-three dollars and seventeen cents," she said slowly.

Carrie was too overwhelmed to speak for a moment. "That's enough for the lease payment, with enough left over for January's utilities and some inventory."

"Enough to keep going," Tanner said quietly.

Shannon turned to Carrie. "They know you're here now. They'll come back."

Carrie looked around at beautiful, now sparsely populated shelves. "We did it."

"You did it," Tanner corrected.

"And the town. All those people!" Shannon said.

"We all did it," Carrie said finally.

Outside, Main Street was quiet, and the glow of streetlights on snow reflected off the wall. Tomorrow was Christmas Eve. The shop would be closed, but she'd drop off a check with the landlord. They would reopen the day after Christmas. More importantly, on December 27, the deadline would pass, and Lamplight Books would still be there.

She thanked Shannon and gave her a hug. She turned to Tanner, beside her, and leaned her head on his shoulder and thanked him. He wrapped an arm around her shoulders and gently kissed her on the forehead.

CHAPTER SIX

DECEMBER 24, Christmas Eve, arrived quietly.

Carrie sat in her empty shop, still stunned by yesterday's success. She'd made her lease payment. She'd saved her business. The town had shown up for her.

And Tanner had left for LA that morning.

After helping her all day yesterday, he got a call from his agent. His meeting was moved up. Who scheduled meetings on Christmas Eve? Apparently, Crescent Gate Studios did. So Tanner was gone.

She tried not to think about him sitting at some gleaming conference table, signing a contract and moving on with his life. Of course, he'd always planned to go home. Her logical brain understood that. But her heart kept reminding her of how right it all felt. They'd all worked together, not as Tanner the actor, but like a team—no, like friends. Except her heart felt more than friendship.

Her phone buzzed.

Shannon: Turn on Channel 7. They're replaying yesterday's footage.

Carrie pulled up the local news on her phone. The station was doing a Christmas Eve special, showing heartwarming stories from the past year. Her shop was featured—footage from yesterday's steady stream of customers and the three of them working together. The community came through for her.

After the Lamplight Books story, they did a follow-up on the charity event. The reporter had done a full investigation into the original scandal.

She'd found the original talk show footage—the unedited version where the actress had unleashed a string of vitriol at Tanner. It was followed by Tanner's response, which, although harsh and defensive, now made so much more sense. The piece quoted sources who'd been present during the rehearsal and described Portia as a demanding narcissist.

Meanwhile, Portia was already backpedaling on social media, claiming it was all a misunderstanding. Her publicist issued a damage control statement. The internet, for once, had turned its attention to the right villain.

Tanner Blake was exonerated.

In the Crescent Gate Studios conference room, twenty-three floors above Los Angeles, Tanner sat across the table from Gregory Wallman, the man who'd discovered three of the last decade's biggest stars. He could make a career with a handshake. The script in front of Tanner was good, and the role was even better —a complex character with real emotional range. It could take his career to the next level.

"We want you," Wallman said simply. "The role is yours if you want it. We start shooting in June, but we need a commitment today." He smiled. "I know the timing isn't ideal, but we've got a narrow window."

Tanner's agent, Laurence, sat beside him, practically vibrating with suppressed excitement. This was five years in the making. It would change everything.

"Can I have a moment?" Tanner asked.

He stepped out and leaned on the balcony railing. Los Angeles lay below him, a vast, glittering sprawl. Somewhere out there was his apartment, his recording studio, and his life—everything he had worked for.

His phone showed three missed calls from Sloane, two from his manager, and texts from friends congratulating him on the hospital video going viral in the right way. The scandal was over. His career was back on track. All he had to do was say yes.

He pulled up Carrie's contact instead. No new messages. She would be at the bookshop, even though it was closed, probably ordering inventory to replace what had sold. The thought of the previous day made him smile.

The door opened behind him. Laurence.

"This is it, Tanner. This is what we've been working toward. That's Gregory Wallman of Crescent Gate, man. Lightning doesn't strike twice."

"I know."

He slapped Tanner's back. "So come on."

Tanner nodded and went back inside with

Laurence. Wallman popped the cork on a bottle of champagne, and they all drank a toast to the project.

CARRIE STOOD in her empty bookshop and looked out the falling snow. Everything had worked out. She was keeping the shop. Tanner was now in his meeting. Even if he didn't get this job, she knew there would be others. He was too talented not to succeed. It was Christmas Eve, and everything was as it should be. So why did her heart ache?

She went home, made some hot chocolate with whipped cream on top, and settled down by the fire with a book. "Merry Christmas, Carrie," she whispered, and she began reading.

Eight hours later, the doorbell rang and startled her from her sleep. She picked up the book that had fallen to the floor, and then stood.

When she opened the door, there he was. Not Tom. Not Santa. Just Tanner Blake, the man who fixed her shelves and her wobbly chair, his jacket dusted with snow, holding two cups of hot chocolate.

"Hi," he said. "Merry Christmas Eve."

An unreasonable amount of joy bubbled up from her heart. "What are you doing here?"

"I got the job." He set the cups on the counter.

Her joy fizzled as quickly as it had come, but she did her best to look happy. "Oh. Well, that's great! Congratulations!"

Tanner nodded. "I sat in that meeting this morning —Christmas Eve, for God's sake!—in a room full of people talking about points and residuals and marketing strategies, and all I could think about was yesterday. You, me, and Shannon, working together. The town showing up. Mrs. Snyder buying seventeen cookbooks." He moved closer. "That was real, the sense of community, the people . . . more than real. It felt like home. And I thought about you. I love how you did what you set out to do."

She smiled, but it felt hollow. Tanner's support meant so much to her—maybe too much. For, in spite of both of them having achieved what they'd hoped for, it meant that their moment together was over. Seeing him this one last time made the pain of losing him harder to hide. She looked at the fire, at the hot chocolate cups—anywhere but his eyes. With one look, she knew she'd betray her true feelings.

"I didn't take it."

"What?" Carrie blinked and looked straight at him, unable to do anything but stare.

His eyes softened as he smiled. "I turned down the job."

"But it's everything you've been working for."

"Yeah, it was. But it's not what I want anymore."

She could barely say, "Why?"

"I found something here that I didn't know I'd longed for. You've built more than a bookstore. It means something to the people here. And you mean something to me."

Carrie reached for the stool by the counter and sat before her knees gave out on her. Tanner was here, which on its own was a bit overwhelming. And he was saying things she didn't dare believe could be true. But what made her heart go weightless was the look in his eyes and the unsteady sound of his voice. It was so unlike the sure, resonant sound she was used to hearing in his recordings.

"As I sat in that meeting, all I could think of, all I wanted, was here. I loved being a part of this life—of your life—not because you need me. You clearly don't. But because I need you."

The vulnerable look in his eyes nearly made her head swim. It was all Carrie could do to think, let alone speak. "But your career—"

"My career is fine. Better than fine, actually. The scandal's blowing over, which means I can get back to work doing what I actually love—reading books. I can narrate from anywhere, even a small town with one bookshop and a lamp in the window." He took her hands in his, stared at them for a moment, then looked into her eyes. "If that bookshop's owner wants me here, that is."

The air left her lungs.

He moved closer. "I want to be part of what you're building here. I want to be part of your life, if you'll have me."

Say something. But she couldn't. All she seemed able to do was gaze numbly. No words would come out.

Tanner went on in that voice that resounded deep down to her soul. "I love how you're able to find just the right book with a particular magic for each child or adult who walks into your shop. And no one organizes sugar packets like you." He flashed that winning smile that always undid her. "But I think it was when you stapled my shirt to the shelf that I knew this was going to be . . . something."

"Once. I stapled you once." Carrie felt her face flush.

"And I've been hooked ever since." His thumb brushed her cheek. "So what do you say? Want a semi-famous voice actor who's good with tools and makes questionable life choices?"

If she had any sense, she'd think this through and realize this could be just a phase. He could come to his senses and go back to LA in a heartbeat, but her heart was beating too loudly to hear herself think. A practical person would be able to see all the ways this could go wrong. But practical was the last thing she was feeling at the moment.

Instead, she softly said words that were etched in her heart, "I have loved you 'against reason, against promise, against peace, against hope, against happiness, against all discouragement that could be.'"

She'd barely finished when Tanner drew her into his arms and kissed her—not gently, not tentatively, but with everything he'd held back since he'd met her. And she kissed him back and unleashed all the passion she'd hidden in her heart, tucked away just for him. His hands combed into her hair, and her back pressed against the counter.

When they broke apart, she said while catching her breath, "So, you're staying?"

He laughed. "I think that's what I've been trying to say. Yes. Yes, I'm staying." He rested his forehead against hers. "I want to fix your shelves. Read to the children at your next hospital fundraiser. Make you coffee every morning. Maybe change up the sugars just to keep you on your toes."

"Oh, I'm on my toes. But we will need a Santa next year."

"Sign me up." He drew her close and kissed her again.

The doorbell rang. Carrie opened the door to find Shannon with a bottle of champagne and a plate of Christmas cookies. "I thought you could use some Christmas Eve company, so I—" She glanced over and saw Tanner. "Oh! Hi." Her eyes went from Carrie to Tanner and back to Carrie again, as if she were watching a tennis match. She then tiptoed to the nearest side table. "So, I'll just set these down here and be on my way. Merry Christmas!" With a wave, she made a dash for the door.

Carrie caught her arm. "No, you're staying."

Shannon wrinkled her face. "Just for a minute."

While Carrie went to the kitchen and got out three champagne flutes, Shannon plopped onto a stool. "So, guys, what's going on? Anything new?" She glanced about expectantly.

TRUE TO HER WORD, Shannon stayed a few minutes and then left for her family's Christmas Eve gathering. Tanner built a fire, and they ordered a pizza and watched *The Shop Around the Corner*.

At midnight, the church bells rang, and snow fell. Tanner pulled her to the window, and they watched it come down, turning Main Street into a sight of pristine, snow-dusted magic.

"Jade was right," he said. "Snow is more beautiful when you've been waiting for it."

"Is that what we were doing? Waiting?"

"I think so. I think we're all waiting until we find home."

She leaned against him, his arms around her, and peace settled in her chest. Peace. Belonging. Home.

"Merry Christmas, Tanner."

"Merry Christmas, Carrie."

Outside, the snow kept falling, and the lamp in the bookshop stayed on, warm and bright. And somewhere in the pediatric wing of Hollydale Hospital, a little girl named Jade looked out her window and smiled at the snow.

EPILOGUE

SIX MONTHS LATER, Lamplight Books was thriving. The publicity from the charity event had brought customers from three counties. Carrie hired two part-time employees, expanded the children's section, and started a weekly story hour that was always packed.

Tanner had converted a bedroom in his upstairs apartment into a recording studio. When he wasn't recording narration, he helped Carrie downstairs in the bookshop. On Thursdays, he volunteered at the hospital, but now there were new children to read to. Hailey was home with her dog, Biscuit. Marco's sister greeted him as he left the hospital for home. Jade made it home in time for the last snow of the season. On the bookshop's Facebook page, she posted a selfie beside the snow fort she'd built.

On a warm June evening, Carrie found Tanner in his studio, recording. She waited until he finished the passage, then she knocked.

As he waved her in, she held up a letter. "This came for you."

She sat down on his desk while he opened and read it.

Dear Mr. Blake,

Thank you for being our Santa. You helped make Christmas special.

We wanted you to know that the hospital is naming the new children's reading room after you: The Tanner Blake Story Corner. It's going to have comfy chairs, lots of books, and a big window so we can all watch the snow.

We hope you'll come read to us there.

Love,

The Kids at Hollydale Children's Hospital

Now smiling, Tanner set down the letter. "They're naming a room after me."

"You earned it."

"*We* earned it. Your event made it happen."

"It all worked out." She lost herself in his gaze.

"I loved every minute of it." He caught her hand and held it. "And I love you."

"I love you too. Even though you leave sawdust everywhere and can't figure out where the coffee filters go."

He squinted. "Because they go in three different places depending on which brand you buy. Your organizational system defies logic."

"It makes perfect sense if you—"

"Shh." He held up a finger, then stood and guided her to his chair. "Sit." He reached for his headphones. "Would you listen to this recording? I'm trying a different approach with this project, and I need your opinion."

She looked skeptical. "Now?"

"It'll just take a minute. Please?"

She sighed but let him settle the headphones over her ears. He leaned over, typed something on his keyboard, and his voice filled her head. That voice. The one she still loved.

"I loved her against reason," he was saying, and she recognized it immediately—the Dickens quote from chapter twenty-nine. The one that made her forget how to breathe. "Against promise, against peace, against hope, against happiness, against all discouragement that could be."

But then he continued, and this wasn't Dickens anymore: "I loved her when she left a light on so the books wouldn't get lonely. I loved her when she refused my help because she needed to prove that she could save herself. And I loved her enough to ask her to marry me."

The recording stopped.

Carrie pulled off the headphones, stunned, still processing what she'd heard. Tanner was on one knee beside the chair.

"Marry me," he said simply. "Let's make this permanent. Let's build a life where I fix your shelves and you fix my broken parts, and we both fix the world a little bit by sharing stories."

She stared at him, her voice gone, her brain still catching up to what was happening.

"Carrie?" He looked suddenly uncertain. "You're supposed to say words now," he prompted.

"You—you recorded a proposal?"

"I narrated it." The corner of his mouth twitched. "I did seventeen takes. That was the best one."

"Seventeen takes of a proposal."

"It's hard to be perfect. You deserve perfect." He was still on one knee, still waiting. "So . . .? Will you?"

"Yes."

He blinked. "Yes?"

"Yes! Yes, I'll marry you. Yes to the shelves and the stories and building a life. Yes to all of it."

He stood, pulled her up, and kissed her. Deep and sure.

THE FOLLOWING CHRISTMAS, they hung a sign in the window:

> *Tell us your Christmas wish.*
> *Your friends at Lamplight Books*

And every day until Christmas, someone did. Because in Hollydale, in a bookshop where the lights never went out, Christmas love was real, and Secret Santa always listened.

THANK YOU!

Thank you for reading! If you enjoyed this book, please consider leaving a review or a rating. Your feedback on bookstore, Goodreads, and Bookbub websites helps other readers discover books they'll enjoy.

instagram.com/jljarvis.writer

facebook.com/jljarvis1writer

x.com/JLJarvis_writer

youtube.com/@jljarvis-author

goodreads.com/jljarvis

bookbub.com/authors/j-l-jarvis

ALSO BY J.L. JARVIS

Waterfront Summers

(Can be read in any order)

The Cottage at Peregrine Cove

The House on Serenity Lake

Moonlight on Mariner's Bluff

Drake & Wilde Mysteries

(Reading Order)

Love in the Time of Pumpkins

Secrets in the Hollow

Shadow of the Horseman

Standalones

(Can be read in any order)

A Cowboy Kind of Love

A Christmas Eve Stop

Christmas by Lamplight

A Kiss in the Rain

App-ily Ever After

Once Upon a Winter

The Red Rose

Highland Vow

Short Stories

(Can be read in any order)

The Magic of Snow

The Eleventh-Hour Pact

A Christmas Yarn

The Farmer and the Belle

Work-Crush Balance

Cedar Creek

(Can be read in any order)

Christmas at Cedar Creek

Snowstorm at Cedar Creek

Sunlight on Cedar Creek

Pine Harbor

(Reading Order)

Allison's Pine Harbor Summer

Evelyn's Pine Harbor Autumn

Lydia's Pine Harbor Christmas

Holiday House

(Can be read in any order)

The Christmas Cabin

The Winter Lodge

The Lighthouse

The Christmas Castle

The Beach House

The Christmas Tree Inn

The Holiday Hideaway

Highland Passage

(Can be read in any order)

Highland Passage

Knight Errant

Lost Bride

Highland Soldiers

(Reading Order)

The Enemy

The Betrayal

The Return

The Wanderer

American Hearts

(Can be read in any order)

Secret Hearts

Forbidden Hearts

Runaway Hearts

For more information, visit jljarvis.com.

Get monthly book news at news.jljarvis.com.

ABOUT THE AUTHOR

J.L. Jarvis is a left-handed former opera singer/teacher/lawyer who writes books. She now lives and writes on a mountaintop in upstate New York.

jljarvis.com

www.ingramcontent.com/pod-product-compliance
Lightning Source LLC
Chambersburg PA
CBHW032109170626
46808CB00008B/2991